Dear Readers,

I apologize for Chester's
behavior in my mouse story.
Sorry for the inconvenience.

Sincerely,
Mélanie Watt

Blah! Blah! Blah!

For ~~Marcos,~~ Eva,
Melina and Layla

For Chester because I couldn't have made this book without him. He's the smartest, most handsome cat in the world. I wish I could be like him someday!

ISBN 978-0-545-34461-6

Text and illustrations copyright © 2007 by Mélanie Watt. All rights reserved. Published by Scholastic Inc., 557 Broadway, New York, NY 10012, by arrangement with Kids Can Press Ltd. SCHOLASTIC and associated logos are trademarks and/or registered trademarks of Scholastic Inc.

12 11 10 9 8 7 6   12 13 14 15 16/0

Printed in the U.S.A.   08

First Scholastic printing, February 2011

The artwork in this book was rendered in pencil and watercolor and was assembled digitally.
The text is set in Carnation and Kidprint.

Edited by Tara Walker
Designed by Mélanie Watt
Author photo by Sophie Gagnon

Chester

NOT Written and illustrated by Mélanie Watt

SCHOLASTIC INC.
New York Toronto London Auckland
Sydney Mexico City New Delhi Hong Kong

Once upon a time there was a mouse.
He lived in a house in the country.

Then Mouse packed
his bags and went
on a trip very, very
far away and we never
saw him ever again!

So Chester moved in
and made a few changes
to HIS new place.

But Mouse returned home.

Oh yes, did I mention he brought back
a really big souvenir with teeth?

Back to the story ...

Once upon a time there was a mouse.

He lived in ... Chester, move out of the way!

...he lived in the country
with his vegetarian dog
who only ate carrots.

Then Mélanie begged
Chester to write a better
story. And it goes something
like this...

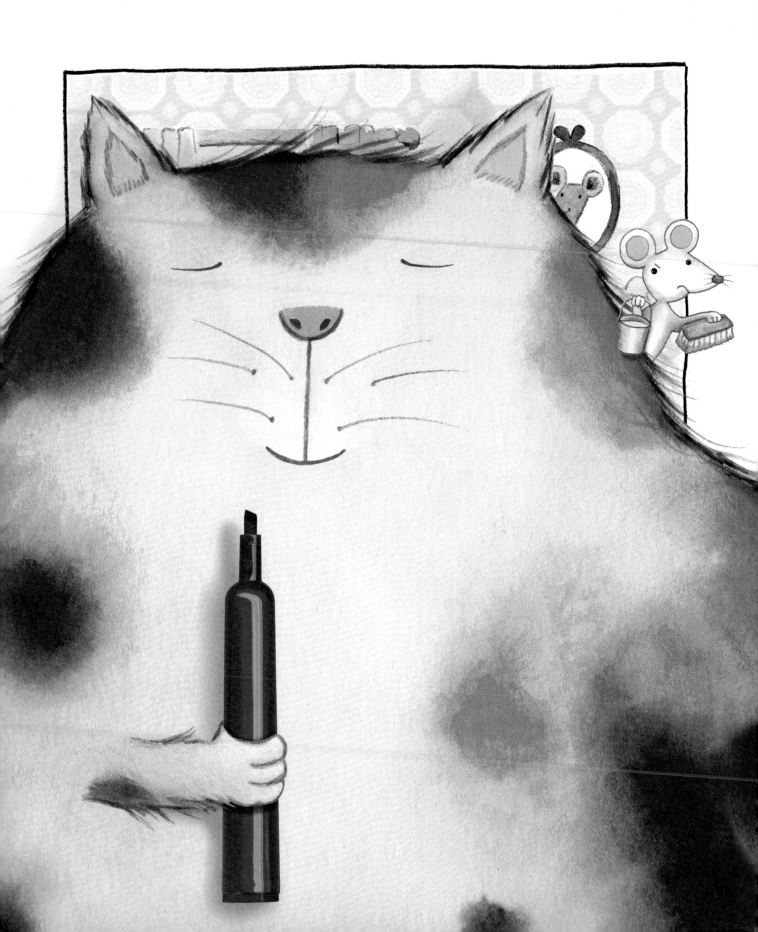

Once upon a time there was ME.
Chester stands for:

Charming
Handsome
Envy of Mouse
Smart
Talented
Envy of Mélanie
Really handsome

Chester lived in Chesterville,
where mice weren't allowed.
It was a beautiful day.

Until it started to rain...

Now, as I was saying ...

Once upon a time there was a mouse.
He lived in a house in the country.

And he lived happily ever after...

Chester!

This is where I draw the line!

Nope!
I'M drawing
the line!

DO NOT cross this line!

Chester! I'm warning you! Hand over the marker and apologize before I count to three!

1...

2...

3 and 4, 5, 6, 7, 8, 9, 10, 11, 12,

13, 14, 15, 16, 17, 18, 19, 20, 21... La! La! La!

All right, Chester!

You want your own story?

You want to be the star of this book?

Well, get ready. Here it is ...

FINALLY!!!

Once upon a time there was a cat named Chester.
He lived in a house in the country.

Chester was a very handsome cat.
Especially when he wore a pink ...

YOU WOULDN'T!!!

NOW it's personal ...